W9-BVB-210

I WANT A DOG

STORY AND PICTURES BY
DAYAL KAUR KHALSA

E

CLARKSON N. POTTER, INC./PUBLISHERS
DISTRIBUTED BY CROWN PUBLISHERS, INC., NEW YORK

ay wanted a dog more than anything else in the world. She thought about dogs all the time. She talked about dogs; she made drawings of dogs; she read books about dogs. The walls of her room were completely covered with pictures of dogs. But every time she asked her parents if she could have a dog, they said, "No."

It seemed as if everyone else in the world had a dog except May. This made her want one even more.

She wanted a dog to play with and to take to the park. She wanted a dog to take care of—to brush and bathe and feed dog biscuits to. But most of all, she wanted to feel the tug of a dog on a leash.

May told her parents that a dog would be good for the whole family.

A dog could chase away robbers, fetch the evening paper, and bring them their slippers. A dog could even be taught to shake hands.

But no matter what reasons she gave, still they always said, "We're sorry, May, but not now. You can have a dog when you're older." May, though, wanted a dog *right now*.

As she sat in school daydreaming about dogs, May had a great idea. If she could show her parents how much dogs were attracted to *her*, maybe they would get her one.

When she got home that afternoon she ran right to the refrigerator and grabbed a thick slice of salami. She went outside and began strolling slowly down the street. Every dog on the block jumped up as May walked by.

By the time she had gone all the way around the block there was a whole herd of hungry dogs trailing behind her. May was very happy. *Ten* dogs!

"They followed me, Ma," she explained when she got home. "Dogs just seem to want to be with me."

Her mother was not fooled. She told May to use the same technique to lead all the dogs back where they belonged.

May was disappointed but not discouraged. She remembered when she had first tried to rollerskate. She kept falling down, but her father told her, "If at first you don't succeed, try, try, try again."

And that's what she had always done. Now she *could* rollerskate. May decided to try another way to get a dog.

For this one she needed to save up all her allowance. When the day she had been planning finally arrived, she went out and bought everything she needed: a birthday cake, candles, a birthday card and—a puppy!

When May got home she set everything up on the kitchen table.

"Ma, come quick!" she yelled. Her mother rushed into the kitchen.

Surprise! Happy Birthday!" May shouted, pointing to a big brown box.
"What can this be?" her mother asked as she pushed the flaps aside.
A little spotted puppy poked his head out and licked her hand.
"I bought you a friend," said May.

At first her mother was too surprised to speak. Then she turned to May, patted her on the shoulder, and said, "Nice try, but not now."

She called a taxi so May could take the puppy right back to the pet store.

May kept repeating to herself, "Try, try, try again."

hat evening her parents decided it was time to settle the dog question once and for all. They sat down in the living room and explained to May why they didn't want her to have a dog now.

Her mother began. "Dogs take a lot of care."

"I'll do it," said May.

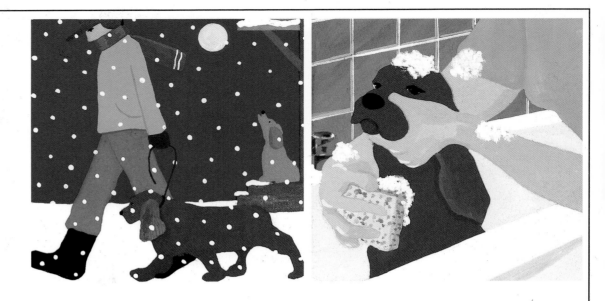

hey have to be walked every morning and every night," her father
said. "In rain and sleet and hail and snow."

"I'll do it," said May.

"Dogs have to be brushed and bathed and taken to the vet for shots,"
her mother said.

"I'll do it," said May.

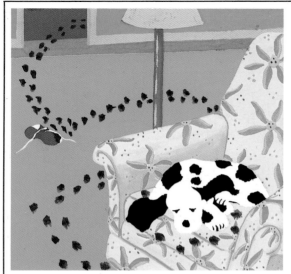  

Dogs have to be trained to obey," said her father.

"I'll do it *all*," said May, for every reason they gave for *not* wanting a dog was exactly why she *did* want a dog.

They had a lot of other reasons as well. Nevertheless, May pleaded, "Please, please, please, *please*, can I have a dog anyway?" But still her parents said, "No."

May was furious. She stomped up to her room, and threw her toys all over the place. She kicked her rollerskate with all her might. It whipped out the door, raced across the hall to the top of the stairs, plunged over, and bumped all the way to the bottom.

May watched in amazement. The rollerskate looked like a little white dog bounding down the stairs.

May had a great idea.

She tied a rope around the rollerskate and pulled. The rollerskate rolled toward her. She walked across the room with it. The rollerskate rolled after her. It was just like walking a dog on a leash.

May went to work. She built a giant training course where she could practice walking her rollerskate.

"We're so happy to see you busy doing something other than always trying to get a dog," her parents told her.

 When she could walk the rollerskate across cracks and around corners without the rollerskate tumbling, May felt ready to try it outside.

The rollerskate bumped over the sidewalk like a frisky little puppy. When May ran fast and stopped short, the rollerskate shot ahead of her, tugging on the leash. It was almost like having a real dog. But when she took her rollerskate to the playground, her friends laughed. They said she looked funny dragging a rollerskate around on a rope.

It's not a rope," she said. "It's a leash. I'm practicing for when I get a real dog. And then I'm only going to let people who *really* know how to walk a dog, walk mine."

After that, they all wanted to walk her rollerskate.

Her rollerskate went with her everywhere. But wherever it said *No Dogs Allowed,* she left it outside, tied to a tree.

On the day the new comic books arrived at Sam's Luncheonette, May could hardly wait to get there. She ran to the store, tossed her rollerskate's leash around a tree, and rushed in.

While she was busy deciding which comic book to buy, outside on the street a big dog trotted up to the rollerskate and began sniffing it all over. He nudged it with his nose.

The leash slipped. He grabbed the roller-skate in his huge mouth and ran away with it.

Imagine how May felt when she came out—and the rollerskate was gone!

She looked for it all over: in doorways, under cars, behind hedges. She stopped people and asked, "Have you seen a rollerskate on a leash?" But no one had.

May felt miserable. It was almost like losing a real dog. She turned toward home, all alone.

Then she remembered those old familiar words: Try, try, try again. So she kept on looking. Even in garbage cans.

She finally found it—scratched and dirty—a block away. She hugged the roller-skate tight and carried it home and cleaned it up just like new.

 fter that, May and her rollerskate were never far apart. She even took it Trick or Treating.

And every day, in rain or sleet or hail or snow, May took her roller-skate for a walk.

Her parents were very impressed. "We can see that when you get a real dog, you'll know how to take good care of it," they said.

In a couple of years, May did get a real dog of her own. Meanwhile, though, May, and all her friends, kept on practicing.

For
Guru Sangat Kaur
and
Sarab Sangeet Singh

Published by Clarkson N. Potter, Inc., 225 Park Avenue South, New York, New York 10003

CLARKSON N. POTTER, POTTER, and colophon are trademarks of Clarkson N. Potter, Inc.

Manufactured in Japan

Library of Congress Cataloging-in-Publication Data

Khalsa, Dayal Kaur.
I want a dog.

Summary: When her parents refuse to get her a dog, May creates an imaginary dog out of a rollerskate.

[1. Dogs—Fiction. 2. Imagination—Fiction]
I. Title.
PZ7.K52647Iab   1987   [E]   86-30329

ISBN 0-517-56532-3

10 9 8 7 6 5 4 3 2 1

First Edition